BEGINNINGS

SNOW WHITE'S
Birthday Wish

BY TESSA ROEHL

ILLUSTRATED BY THE
DISNEY STORYBOOK ART TEAM

SCHOLASTIC
SYDNEY AUCKLAND NEW YORK TORONTO LONDON MEXICO CITY
NEW DELHI HONG KONG BUENOS AIRES PUERTO RICO

FOR MILO.

Published by Scholastic Australia in 2021.

Scholastic Australia Pty Limited
PO Box 579 Gosford NSW 2250
ABN 11 000 614 577
www.scholastic.com.au

Part of the Scholastic Group
Sydney • Auckland • New York • Toronto • London • Mexico City
New Delhi • Hong Kong • Buenos Aires • Puerto Rico

ISBN 978-1-76112-572-0

Printed in China.

Scholastic Australia's policy, in association with its printers, is to use papers that are
renewable and made efficiently from wood grown in responsibly managed forests, so as to
minimise its environmental footprint.

10 9 8 7 6 5 4 3 2 1   21 22 23 24 25 / 2

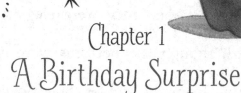

Chapter 1
A Birthday Surprise

Snow White held out an apple for Frost. She'd snuck a few off the table at breakfast, hoping the sweet red fruit would appeal to the horse. Snow had seen Benjamin, the stable boy, offering apples to her before. But Frost kept her eyes towards the stall door, as though anything happening outside would be more interesting than the princess inside, who was trying to pay the horse a visit.

Boots appeared under the door. Snow knew those boots: they were elegant and polished, though the bottoms were caked with mud from the stables. She looked up and saw her father, the king, peering down at her. He raised an eyebrow.

'I thought you might be here. I heard that Cook made you a special birthday breakfast, but you only ate two bites of it.'

'I wanted to say good morning to Frost and the other horses,' Snow answered, coming out of the stall to talk to her father.

'Well, Frost seems quite pleased to be included in the celebrations,' the king said, chuckling. Frost was still ignoring Snow, despite the apple in the princess's hand.

Snow put the piece of fruit back in the pocket of the apron she wore to keep her dress clean when visiting the stables. 'I wish that were true.'

Benjamin approached the stall and bowed slightly in greeting the king. 'Your Majesty,' he said. The boy, who was several years older than Snow, tossed fresh hay into

Frost's stall. The moment Frost saw him, she perked up. The horse's ears twitched and she snorted, twisting her head to get closer to Benjamin. 'And good morning to you, too, girl,' he said to Frost, giving her an affectionate rub on the neck. Frost closed her eyes in satisfaction, snorting again.

Snow sighed. 'Oh, hello, Princess,' Benjamin said. 'I didn't see you there.'

'Hello, Benjamin. I'm not so sure Frost did, either.' Snow watched the stable boy finish with the hay. So did Frost. Even though Snow White was the princess, Frost clearly thought of Benjamin as royalty.

'How do you do it?' Snow asked.

'Do what?' Benjamin replied, dusting off his hands and playfully moving Frost's head out of the way so he could see Snow better.

'How did you get her to like you so much? I've been trying and trying, and . . .' She looked up at her father. 'It's no use.'

'Oh, come now,' her father said. 'I'm sure that's not true. Animals love you, darling.'

'*Most* of them do.' *But not this horse*, Snow thought.

Snow had a special talent for finding lost and injured animals: a baby bird who'd fallen from his nest, a chipmunk with a broken leg, a fawn who'd strayed too far from her forest home. Every single one had spent time at the castle, being nursed back to health by Snow.

Yes, the bird had given the cook a fright once his wings healed and he decided to fly around the kitchen. And her father was cross when he found the chipmunk gnawing on the arm of his throne. And Benjamin's father, Klaus, the stable master, was startled to find a young deer napping in the stables. But Snow always managed to make them understand that she simply had to help the animals.

'Maybe you should sing for Frost, Princess,' Benjamin suggested. 'I hear that goes over well.'

The king cleared his throat.

Snow was pretty certain Benjamin was teasing her, because she'd been shooed out of various rooms in the castle for singing a little loudly a little too often, distracting everyone from the serious business that went on there. But in any case . . . 'I tried that already. She was not interested,' replied Snow.

Benjamin chuckled and started to move on to the next stall. 'Benjamin,' the king said, 'I've come down here with a message for Snow that concerns you as well. Stick around for a moment.'

Benjamin stopped immediately. 'Yes, Your Majesty.'

'Darling,' the king said to Snow, 'this year for your birthday, I'm letting you choose your own gift.'

'You are?' Snow asked, surprised.

'I think it's about time you choose a horse to be your own,' the king said.

'Oh, Father! What a wonderful gift. Thank you so much!' Snow jumped with excitement. Ever since she could remember, her father had told her that once she was old enough, she would get her own horse. The day she'd dreamed of had finally arrived!

The king continued: 'The question is, which horse would you like? Benjamin and Klaus will continue to care for her, of course, but the one you choose will be all yours . . . to ride, to bond with, to race . . .'

Snow grimaced. For years, her father had held the title to almost every horse race in the kingdom and beyond. There was a reason his horse was named Champion. To Snow White's dismay, he expected her to share his passion for racing. While she loved riding horses, she preferred a lazy walk over the castle grounds or a casual trot in the meadow. She didn't have the heart to tell her father how terrified she was by the idea of riding a horse at high speeds. What drew her to the animals in the stables and the woods was how much she loved them—not what they could do for her, like win a race.

'So, I can choose any horse?' Snow asked.

'Any horse,' her father answered. 'Though I have a feeling I know which one that will be.' He winked at his daughter.

The king was talking about Frost. Snow looked at the horse and noticed that

Benjamin, his face serious, was staring at the animal, too. It did seem like Frost was the ideal match for Snow. She was elegant and grand, with a name that evoked the sparkling winter. And of course, she was the perfect breed for racing. But Frost had never shown an interest in Snow. No matter how much Snow tried to bond with the horse, Frost paid her no mind.

'Any horse. Hmmm . . .' Snow smiled. 'I might like to take Champion out for a test ride, in that case. Benjamin, could you saddle him up for me?'

Benjamin looked shocked, and Snow's father turned as white as Frost's coat.

'Snow, I don't . . .' The king trailed off, searching for words.

'Father, I'm only kidding!' The king and Benjamin let out nervous laughs.

Snow giggled. Frost was shoving her nose into Benjamin's hand. 'I think I should take some time to make up my mind. You always say to make decisions thoughtfully and weigh all options.'

The king nodded. 'That I do.'

'It's a big decision,' Snow said. 'I'll have to think about it.'

'That's my girl,' the king said, and kissed his daughter on the forehead. 'Now, I'll go check on Champion before you get any more ideas.' He left, disappearing into another part of the stables.

'I was sure Frost would be your choice right away,' Benjamin said, eyeing the princess curiously. 'She's certainly going to be the best racehorse in the kingdom.'

'Frost likes you better than she likes me. I don't think she'd even want to be my horse.' Snow almost choked up. Until she said it out loud, she hadn't realised how much she felt this was true.

Benjamin shook his head. 'Nah, that's just because I feed her and see her every day. I'm sure if you came around more, she'd act the same with you.'

'I've been here every day for months!' Snow exclaimed.

'Oh, right.' Benjamin stroked Frost behind the ears. 'Still, she's something special. Why, if I had a chance to have a horse like this . . .'

Snow knew he was right. Frost had to be the one. It made the most sense. But something in her wasn't ready to choose just yet.

She needed to clear her head. So, Snow decided to take a walk.

Chapter 2
The Wishing Well

Snow White took off her apron and set out across the grassy fields towards the inner gardens of the castle. She took her time, thinking things over as she made her way to a special place: the wishing well.

She knew her father hoped that having a horse of her own would distract her from bringing other animals home. While she didn't plan to give up helping injured creatures, she *was* looking forward to bonding with an animal who didn't have to return to the wild once healed—who would truly be a friend forever. But if not Frost, then which horse would be the right fit?

Snow loved all the royal horses dearly, but none seemed like the right match. There was the set of ponies, Doppel and Ganger, that Snow had learned to ride when she was smaller. They were gentle, silky and sweet. But Snow didn't know how she could choose one over the other. They might as well have been identical twins.

Then there was Horace, a very silly creature. Snow didn't think he realised that he was a *royal* horse. Disobeying Klaus's instructions, he always made Snow giggle. He was mostly interested in playing with the other horses and humans.

And then there was Gertrude, a sweet grey mare Snow thought might be even older than her tutor, who was very old indeed. Gertrude was always nuzzling Snow affectionately and listened to her songs attentively, but Snow had the feeling that Gertrude wouldn't want to go on many rides or forest adventures.

The sight of the wishing well in the middle of the courtyard lifted Snow's spirits. No matter what troubles she had, the well was a place she could sing out her sorrows and her dreams, putting them in the hands of the mysterious force that made wishes come true.

She glanced around to make sure no-one was near. All she could see, other than the castle itself, was the wall that bordered the courtyard and the great forest beyond. Satisfied that she was alone, Snow leaned her elbow on the stone rim of the well, thinking. Part of making this wish was going to be knowing what exactly she wanted to wish for.

The princess had long dreamed of having Frost as her very own, not just to ride and care for but—even more important—to be her companion. Someone to play with and fill

the days. Someone to help her feel less lonely when her father was on important business and the castle attendants were tired of her singing. But Snow wasn't sure that Frost wanted the same thing.

Snow bit her lip. She began, hoping the right words for the right wish would come to her.

'*I'm wishing,*' Snow sang. She always started this way, to make sure the well was listening. Her father had once told her that if you heard the well echo, that meant the wish would come true.

The well echoed in a sweet watery voice: '*I'm wishing.*'

She continued, *'For—'*

Crack!

Before she could even think about her next words, the sound came from beyond the wall. *Just an animal out for a walk*, she thought, trying to shake it off and return to her wish.

She began again. *'I'm wishing,'* she sang. But any answer the well might have given was smothered by a snap and shifting trees.

Someone, or some*thing*, in the forest wanted Snow's attention.

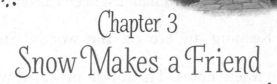

Chapter 3
Snow Makes a Friend

Snow unlocked the small gate and crept beyond the courtyard wall towards the forest. She'd always been interested in the woods outside her castle home. They were wild and surprising, different from the tidy grounds of the castle. She'd walked through the forest several times with her father and had always felt that there were mysteries waiting to be discovered, stories waiting to be told.

But now the forest seemed still. Perhaps the sounds she'd heard had just been the wind.

Keeping an eye on the woods, Snow sang a few notes. The forest answered with another loud crunch. This time she saw the trees rustling. Was it a bird? A woodcutter? A rabbit? She sang another note, and the trees moved again. Whatever was there, it was reacting to her voice. *Perhaps it's a magic tree*, Snow thought as she neared the woods.

But when she reached the trees, Snow didn't see anything: no person, no rabbit or squirrel, no tree with a friendly, magical face. She took a few careful steps into the forest. The sunlight looked different under the thick treetops. The area was dark and shadowy, but dreamy and peaceful at the same time.

Snow continued walking and began to sing again. To her left, a bush moved. She turned and approached warily. There she saw what had been making the commotion. It was no small creature—it was a horse!

'Oh my!' Snow gasped. The horse, lying on the ground, responded with a whinny.

'How on earth are you making all that noise?' she asked.

The horse was resting among the pine needles, one leg under the trunk of a thin tree. He pressed his hoof against the bark, and Snow saw that this was enough to bend the trunk so the upper branches jostled the other trees nearby, causing other branches to snap and break.

'You sure are a smart one,' Snow said as she moved closer to the animal. She was cautious. She had experience rescuing animals, but she'd never handled a wild horse, and she knew to be careful with a scared creature.

'Did you hear me singing?' Snow asked. The horse snorted, which Snow thought meant yes.

'You wanted to get my attention?'

Another snort.

'Well, it worked.' Snow was almost close

enough to touch the animal now . . . and she didn't like what she saw. All her life she'd been around royal horses or horses who belonged to villagers or farmers in town— healthy, strong working horses. So, she could tell that something was wrong with this one. She could see his bones through his grey coat. Patches of hair were missing. His eyes were sad but still alert. And then Snow saw the most alarming thing of all: a wound on his rump, right near the top of his tail.

Snow pointed at the gash. 'Does that hurt?' she asked.

The horse met her eyes with a look that said it did hurt—very much.

Snow fished in her pocket for an apple and held it out to the horse. He took the apple in his teeth so he could eat it. As he chewed, Snow noticed a patch of white hair in the shape of a crescent moon on his forehead.

'If you can be patient and stay here for a bit longer, I'll come back with some help for you,' Snow said. The horse stayed focused on the apple.

'I'll even bring you another apple,' Snow added. The horse glanced up at her this time and gave her a slow blink, seeming to tell her that he would wait.

That was all Snow needed. She quickly ran out of the forest, through the gate, through the courtyard and down to the stables to find help.

'Father!' Snow called as she burst into the stables.

Benjamin emerged from one of the stalls. 'Whoa there, Princess. Everything okay?'

'There's an injured horse in the forest. Where's my father? Or yours?' Snow asked, her voice full of worry.

Benjamin's usual smirk vanished. 'They're out grooming Champion,' he said.

Snow and Benjamin ran to the post outside, where Champion was tethered. Klaus and the king were brushing the muscular horse's coal-black coat. Snow quickly explained to the men what she'd found in the woods. 'He needs our help,' she finished.

'Klaus will fetch supplies,' her father said. 'Come, show us where to find him.'

Her father hoisted Snow up onto Champion and sat behind her. As they galloped towards the forest, with Klaus and Benjamin on Horace and Gertrude not far behind, Snow felt a rush of relief. The wounded horse would be in good hands now.

The small party trotted through the forest to where the horse lay. As Champion and the other two horses got close, Snow saw

the injured horse's nostrils flare. She knew

that meant he was uneasy.

'May I go first?' Snow asked her father.

'To tell him you're friends?'

The king eyed the horse and then his

daughter. He dismounted Champion, then

helped Snow down. 'All right, but be careful.

Wild animals, especially when hurt, can be

unpredictable.'

Snow moved towards the horse slowly. She held out another apple, and the horse's eyes fixated on it. 'See? Just as I promised,' she said. His weary body shivered as she reached out her other hand to stroke the crescent moon on his forehead. 'I've brought some people to help you. You can trust them. They're going to take care of you.' The horse's eyes tore away from the apple as she spoke. They were big, round and tired, and he seemed to accept her words. Snow gave him the apple and, as he chewed, she waved the others over.

Klaus, with Benjamin's help, began to clean the horse's wound. 'It's not so bad,

Princess,' Klaus said. 'Looks much nastier than it is. He just scraped himself on something.'

Snow's father watched the horse eat the apple. 'He must have been a beautiful creature once,' the king said.

'Why, he's a beautiful creature now, Father. Beauty isn't just on the outside, you know,' Snow said. 'You can tell his spirit is strong. We have to bring him back home.'

The king considered it. 'Darling, this horse is not like the other animals you've rescued. He's not an injured tortoise or bluebird.'

'He needs us, Father. He needs a home.'

'Snow, he may be wild, in which case he would require a lot of special attention. Or he may have escaped from another home, in which case he ought to be returned.'

'Whether he came from the wild or another home, he isn't well,' Snow said softly. 'Please, Father. We can't leave him here.'

Her father examined the horse again. Snow could tell that he wasn't convinced. 'I don't know . . .'

'I choose him as my horse,' Snow White said firmly.

The king, Klaus and Benjamin looked at Snow in surprise.

'You do?' Benjamin exclaimed. His father shushed him.

'This is the horse I want for my birthday gift. I've made my choice,' Snow said. She understood now why she had been so uncertain about choosing Frost. There had been another horse waiting for her. One who needed her. He nuzzled the princess's knee and nickered.

The king furrowed his brow. 'He's not like the royal horses, who are disciplined and already trained. He'll be a challenge. Are you sure you're up for the work involved?'

'I'm sure,' Snow said confidently.

'We'll need to check around to make sure no-one is missing a horse'—her father sighed—'but otherwise, consider him yours.'

Snow beamed. She was sure the horse had come to this spot for a reason: to find her. He couldn't belong to someone else. She leaned over to hug the horse's neck. As she did, her eyes fell upon the crescent marking. 'Moonsilver,' she whispered into the horse's ear. 'I'll call you Moonsilver.'

Chapter 4
Moonsilver Comes Home

The journey back to the stables was slow and careful. Snow walked the injured horse, clutching the rope tied loosely around his neck. The king, Klaus and Benjamin rode in a cluster around them, keeping watch. Snow felt Moonsilver was being very brave.

At the stables, Klaus and Benjamin quickly dismounted Horace and Gertrude and led them away, along with Champion.

Snow's father walked around Moonsilver, sizing him up. 'With some meat on his bones, he could be a good-sized stallion.' The king stood back, frowning at one of the larger hairless patches on Moonsilver's haunch. 'But, darling, are you sure Frost isn't a better match for you? She's of the best breeding, she's well trained and she's already familiar with you. We know where she came from . . .'

'Father,' Snow whispered, 'you shouldn't speak like that in front of Moonsilver. It's not polite.'

'What?' her father asked. He looked confused.

'Moonsilver,' Snow repeated, pointing at the grey horse.

'Ah,' the king said. 'You've named him already.'

Snow reached out to rub Moonsilver's ears. 'Of course!'

'Of course,' the king repeated, frowning.

When Klaus and Benjamin returned, Benjamin gestured for Snow to hand him Moonsilver's rope. 'Where are you taking him?' she asked.

'We'll get him cleaned up, Princess,' Klaus answered. 'He could use a good scrubbing before he settles in to rest.'

'I'll do it,' Snow volunteered. Benjamin

laughed but quieted instantly when his father shot him a glare.

'I can!' she insisted.

'I'm sure you can, Princess,' Klaus replied, but he was looking at Snow's father.

The king motioned to Klaus and Benjamin, and they led Moonsilver away to the stables.

'But, Father—' Snow began to protest.

'Take one ride on Frost,' her father said.

'I've ridden Frost before. I've chosen Moonsilver,' Snow said.

'I just want you to feel some of Frost's speed,' her father said. 'Come out for a gallop with me and Champion. Afterwards, if you'd still rather have Moonsilver as your horse, I won't stand in your way.'

Snow was torn. She never wanted to pass up special time with her father, but she wished it didn't have to involve horse racing. 'Could I just make sure Moonsilver is okay before we go?' Snow asked.

'All right,' her father said. 'I'll get Frost saddled up for you.'

Snow ran to Klaus and Benjamin, who had already begun brushing Moonsilver with soapy water. Snow could tell Moonsilver wasn't happy about it, but he was tolerating it. The water collecting at his hooves was almost black with dirt as the forest was

washed away in a stream of leaves, brambles and mud. Snow grabbed a sponge from the bucket and began to scrub Moonsilver's neck gently.

'Klaus and Benjamin are your friends,' she whispered to the horse. 'I'm going out with my father for a bit, but I'll come back and check on you soon. Okay?'

Moonsilver's ears pointed back and he nickered.

'You don't have to worry,' Snow said. 'You're my family now.'

Snow and her father trotted across the sweeping castle grounds—Snow on Frost and the king on Champion. The ride on the white horse was exactly how it always was: graceful, smooth and elegant.

Snow enjoyed riding Frost and she'd always admired the mare, but she just didn't feel the same bond with her that she felt with Moonsilver. Moonsilver felt right, somehow. Like they belonged together.

When Snow and her father reached the open fields, with plenty of room to gallop, the king set a brisker pace. He instructed Snow to move Frost faster by leaning her body forwards. Frost easily shifted from a walk to a trot and then to a canter, increasing in speed to keep up with Champion. Snow had spent enough time with animals—enough time with Frost herself—to tell that the horse was having the time of her life. Frost loved being out there as much as the king and Champion did.

But Snow did not.

Frost began to gallop to keep up with Champion. Snow's hands turned white as she gripped Frost's reins. Her eyes stung from the whipping wind, and her breath stuck in her throat.

The faster they rode, the more Snow just wanted it to end so she could be back at the stables, safe on the ground.

She pulled back on the reins the way her father had taught her. Ever the dutiful horse,

Frost slowed to a stop. Champion and the king galloped on for a few moments before they realised Snow and Frost had fallen behind. The king and his black steed turned around and trotted back.

'Everything all right?' he asked. 'A little too fast?'

Snow gulped. *Much more than a little*, she thought. She still hadn't the heart to tell him that the thing he loved made her miserable.

'We'll get there yet,' he said. 'Let's head back now.'

They trotted towards the stables. Snow relaxed, enjoying the ride now that she felt comfortable with the pace.

Snow noticed that far off in the distance, a figure stood outside the stables. It was Benjamin. But as they got closer, he turned back to his chores—almost as though he didn't want them to know he'd been watching.

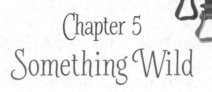

Chapter 5
Something Wild

At the stables, Klaus and Benjamin helped Snow down from Frost. Klaus led Frost away while the king hopped off Champion.

'How was the ride?' Benjamin asked.

'It was . . . exciting,' Snow said, brushing her skirts.

'Any more thoughts about what I said earlier?' her father asked as he removed Champion's saddle.

Snow didn't want to hurt her father's feelings. 'I love Frost. I do. But . . .'

'Say no more,' her father replied. He put his hand on her shoulder. 'As I said, we'll have to make sure Moonsilver doesn't already have a home. But if he doesn't, he's all yours.'

With that, he led Champion away, leaving Snow with Benjamin.

'Are you *sure* you're making the right decision?' Benjamin asked once the king was out of sight.

'I'm sure,' Snow said. 'What's the matter? You don't like Moonsilver?'

'Moonsilver?' Benjamin rolled his eyes at

the name. 'Liking doesn't have anything to do with it. That horse has seen some better days.'

'And now that he's with us, he'll see even *more* better days,' Snow said.

They walked together to Moonsilver's stall, where the horse was snacking on hay.

'How old do you think he is?' Snow asked Benjamin as they watched him gulp down a mouthful.

'From the length of his teeth, I'd guess he's about seven years old,' Benjamin said, squinting at Moonsilver's mouth. 'But the rest of him looks like he's been wandering around forever.'

'You'll see,' Snow said. 'He'll be just as shiny and fresh and healthy as the rest of these horses in no time.'

Benjamin stayed quiet, which was unusual for him. He almost always had *something* to say.

'Are you upset because there's another horse to care for now?' Snow asked.

'I'm not worried about that,' Benjamin said.

'I promise I'll do the work,' Snow said. 'It will be like he isn't even here.'

'And maybe he won't be,' Benjamin muttered as he stepped away from the stall.

'What do you mean?' Snow asked.

'I tried saddling him up while you were out with your father. He wouldn't let me get anywhere near him. He's *wild*, Princess.' Benjamin reached his hand over the stall. Moonsilver backed away, nostrils flaring, ears flattened, eyes wide. He pawed the ground with his front hoof.

'That's a good thing, right? That means there's less chance that he has another

owner somewhere,' Snow said. But she didn't like what she was seeing. Moonsilver had been so gentle with her. So instantly trusting. So instantly kind. With Benjamin he was instantly . . . not those things.

Benjamin pulled his hand away from Moonsilver. The horse stayed in the corner, eyeing Benjamin warily for several moments, until he felt safe enough to return to the hay.

'Wild horses aren't used to being in stalls, Princess,' Benjamin said. 'They're used to eating what they want, doing what they want, going wherever they want. Don't be surprised if that horse is gone by tomorrow morning.'

'But surely he can't escape.' Snow glanced around the stables. 'He's in a safe place now. He has food; he has shelter. He wouldn't leave even if he could.' *Would he?* Snow wondered.

Benjamin folded his arms. 'I'm just saying: don't get too attached to Moonriver.'

'Moon*silver*,' Snow said, correcting him. She hoped Benjamin was wrong. Moonsilver had wanted her to find him; she was sure of it. He *needed* her. 'What can we do?' she asked.

'Well . . .' Benjamin scratched his head. 'The only way to make him not wild is to tame him.'

'He's tame with me,' Snow said.

'No,' Benjamin said. '*Real* taming. Not just being nice to get apples. You need to create a true bond, where the horse knows you're his master.'

Snow wanted a true bond. She wasn't sure about the master stuff, but if her bond with Moonsilver wasn't yet true, she definitely wanted it to be.

'You know how to do that?' Snow asked.

'Plenty of the villagers have managed to tame wild horses. I've spent some time helping them out when things are slow up here.'

'Can you teach us?' Snow asked.

'Definitely,' Benjamin said. 'Getting this horse up to royal standards would be a good thing for all of us. It will help show your father what I can do.'

Snow noticed, though, that as Benjamin spoke, he was looking at Frost and not Moonsilver. She threw her arms around the stable boy, catching him off guard.

'Thank you, thank you!' she cried. 'I'll meet you back here first thing in the morning.'

Chapter 6
Training

During breakfast the next day, Snow was bursting with excitement. She couldn't wait to run down to the stables to see how Moonsilver's first night had been. Unfortunately, her father insisted she finish at least half her eggs before she was dismissed.

'Moonsilver needs time to eat his breakfast, too,' the king added.

'Benjamin should wait for me to feed

him,' Snow said. 'I told him I would do all the work.'

'I've sent a messenger to ask about Moonsilver in all the nearby villages,' her father said as he sipped his tea. 'He should have an answer when he returns in a few days. Be careful not to get too attached until then.'

'Benjamin is sure that Moonsilver is wild,' Snow said. 'He's going to show me how to train him.'

'So you don't want racing lessons from your old papa anymore?' her father said. 'Just because you've taken on this . . . less fortunate horse instead of Frost, it doesn't mean you have to give up on racing. It may just take a bit longer to whip Moonsilver into shape.'

'Right . . .' Snow said. She hoped it was long enough for her father to completely forget about her racing. 'But I know you're busy. In the meantime, Benjamin and I will work on the training. You'll see— Moonsilver and I will be as much a pair as you and Champion.'

'I expect nothing less,' her father said. 'Now go on and get started.'

When she reached the stables, Snow waved a quick hello to Klaus, who was shovelling out some muck. She ran straight for Moonsilver's stall and was relieved to see that the horse was still there. 'I'm glad you didn't run away,' she told him.

'He's much better than he was yesterday,' Klaus said, joining Snow. 'The wound is healing up nicely.'

'Is he safe to ride yet?' Snow asked the stable master.

Klaus rubbed his chin thoughtfully. 'Safe for him? As long as he doesn't go too far. But keep in mind that we don't know if this horse has been ridden before. I'm not sure it would be safe for *you*.'

'Benjamin will help,' Snow said. 'Where is he?'

'Gathering up the morning meals,' Klaus said, motioning towards the bales of hay outside the stables.

Snow ran to find Benjamin. He was loading hay into a small wagon, preparing to take it around to the horses.

'Let me help,' Snow said. She scooped a giant armful of hay and placed it in the wagon. It scratched her arms and poked through the light linen of her dress. She smiled, thinking about how this hay would be Moonsilver's breakfast.

Snow plucked one piece of hay from the wagon. She held it up to her nose and sniffed, then took a delicate bite. It tasted a bit like

the driest of dry toast, which was sometimes served for breakfast when the regular cook was on holidays. The hay also had a touch of sweetness to it. Snow figured Moonsilver liked that, considering how fond he was of apples.

'What are you *doing*?' Benjamin asked.

Snow looked up. Benjamin was staring at her with his mouth hanging wide open.

'What?' she asked. 'All these years feeding this to the animals and you've never tried it?'

'Of course not!' he exclaimed.

'Why not?' she asked.

'Because I'm a *human* and I eat *human food*,' he said, shaking his head as he began to push the wagon into the stables.

'I think it will help me get inside Moonsilver's mind—to know what he's eating, what he's seeing, what he's hearing, what he's feeling.' She watched Benjamin toss hay into the stalls. She grabbed another pitchfork and did the same. With two of them doing the job, the work would be done twice as fast, and then Benjamin would be able to start helping her with Moonsilver.

'What you need to be thinking about is how to get him to obey you,' Benjamin said.

Snow tossed the last of the hay to Champion, who took a dignified bite. 'I'm ready to learn when you're ready to teach.'

Benjamin walked to Moonsilver's stall and swung the door open. Moonsilver was grazing on the hay already. Snow was happy to see his appetite was strong.

'First things first. Let's get him out of the stall.'

'Come on, Moonsilver,' Snow said, beckoning him to move forwards. His eyes moved up as she spoke, but he didn't lift his head from the hay.

'Oh, I know!' she said. 'He loves apples. If I get one—'

'You can't rely on bribing him,' Benjamin said. 'We have to be firm, let him know that we're in charge.' He stood next to Snow, facing the horse. 'Moonsilver,' he boomed in a loud, deep voice.

Still munching the hay, Moonsilver looked at Benjamin, then at Snow. Snow nodded at the horse and he raised his head.

'You see?' Benjamin said. 'You have to be firm.' He grabbed a halter and showed Snow how to put it on, making sure to approach from the side. 'Horses have blind spots—places where it's hard for them to see you. If you approach him straight on, it can scare him. And we don't need to be startling any wild horses.'

'No,' Snow agreed. She reached for the horse's lead in his hand.

'Not yet,' Benjamin said. 'Let's see how well he follows me before we let you try. I have to keep you safe.'

Disappointed, Snow put her hands into her apron pocket. Benjamin started towards the stable exit where the troughs and buckets were. Moonsilver didn't follow. Instead, the horse turned towards the opposite exit: the one that led towards the forest where Snow had found him the day before.

Benjamin used his firm voice again. 'Come.'

Moonsilver didn't budge. Snow stifled a giggle. 'Should I get an apple?' she asked. Moonsilver's ears flicked at her words.

'We don't need *apples*,' Benjamin grumbled. 'We just need him to listen.'

'Apples later, then,' Snow said to Moonsilver, '*after* you've finished your lessons.'

'Moonsilver, *come*,' Benjamin said again in his most serious voice yet. Moonsilver finally walked towards Benjamin and Snow. They continued leading him out of the stables and towards the riding pen, a large fenced-off circle in the meadow.

'I think he understood me,' Snow said to Benjamin.

'I think he understood my demand for respect,' Benjamin responded. 'You can't be too gentle, Princess. Horses want to understand us, but they speak a different language than we do. We have to show them who's boss.' Benjamin led Moonsilver and Snow into the pen, latching the gate behind them.

'I don't want to be mean,' Snow said.

Benjamin let the lead drop from his hands. Moonsilver stood still. 'Well, you certainly shouldn't be *mean*. Do you know what horses do when they're scared?'

Snow shook her head.

'When animals get scared,' Benjamin continued, 'some will fight, but others will run. Horses are runners. It's in their nature. Especially the wild ones.' He pointed over his shoulder at the fence. 'That should keep him from running away, as long as he's not a jumper, too.'

Snow frowned. She hoped Moonsilver

wouldn't want to run away at all—not just because the pen was keeping him in. 'So what now?'

Benjamin puffed out his chest. 'I'm going to try riding him.'

'Already?' Snow asked.

'We won't know if it's possible until we try.' Benjamin shrugged.

Snow decided to stand outside the pen, but she stayed close to Benjamin and Moonsilver.

'Whoa, boy,' Benjamin said as he advanced towards the horse. 'You should use your words when nearing a horse who isn't looking at you,' he said to Snow. 'You don't want to frighten him.' Moonsilver glanced at Snow, then shifted his gaze to Benjamin and lifted his back leg, pawing at the ground.

'I don't think he likes this,' Snow said.

'Nope,' Benjamin answered. 'That's a warning sign. Easy, boy.' Benjamin held out his hands. Moonsilver flattened his ears. Snow thought he looked angry.

'Moonsilver, it's all right,' Snow called out. Moonsilver's ears relaxed.

Then, faster than Snow or Moonsilver could react, Benjamin ran up to the horse

and hopped onto his back. Moonsilver stepped backwards, confused by the strange new weight on his body.

'Gotcha!' Benjamin shouted.

Moonsilver began to run in circles around the edge of the pen. It frightened Snow. Moonsilver was clearly in distress and Benjamin did not look secure.

And sure enough, after a few moments of Moonsilver speeding around the pen, Benjamin soon fell off the horse and landed on his backside—*hard*.

Chapter 7
Back on the Horse

'Oh, no!' Snow cried. She was about to climb back into the pen when Benjamin stood up and held out his hand, motioning for her to stop.

'I expected this!' Benjamin shouted. 'I'm fine. It's okay.'

But it didn't seem okay to Snow. Benjamin could have been seriously hurt. Moonsilver was keeping his distance from the boy, nervously trotting back and forth. Snow wanted to put a stop to the training— but what could she say? Benjamin was the horse expert.

Benjamin very cautiously approached Moonsilver once more. The horse avoided him, moving in the other direction. Benjamin followed. They continued the chase until Benjamin rushed forwards and jumped onto the horse again. Moonsilver bucked about, trying to dislodge the person on his back.

Benjamin fell hard—again.

'Benjamin!' Snow called out. Moonsilver went to the other side of the pen. Benjamin

rose to his feet. 'I
think you should
take a break!'
Snow said.

The stable boy

dusted off his trousers. 'I'm showing him
who's boss, Princess!' he shouted back to her,
laughing. 'Better I get scraped up than you,
right?'

He jogged to
Moonsilver. *No*,
Snow thought. It
wasn't better. She
didn't want *anyone*
to get scraped

up! Snow glanced back towards the stables.
Klaus was raking the hay, not paying any
attention to them.

Moonsilver trotted around the edge
of the pen. Snow could see in the way
the horse moved his
body—flicking his tail,
twitching his ears—
that he was nervous.
Snow felt that if she
could just somehow tell him that Benjamin
was only trying to help, Moonsilver would
understand. 'Look at me,' Snow whispered,
and waved to the horse to get his attention.

To Snow's surprise, Moonsilver turned

his head towards her. Snow smiled at him, and his body relaxed. His ears tilted forward, and he lifted his head high. Moonsilver was so distracted by Snow that he didn't notice Benjamin creeping towards him from the side. Snow couldn't help yelling, 'No!' before Benjamin could take another leap at the horse.

As soon as the shout escaped Snow's lips, Moonsilver startled and bolted towards her, knocking Benjamin over.

Snow ran to Benjamin. 'Are you all right?' she asked when she reached him.

Benjamin just glared up at her, his eyes blazing. He was holding his left arm tenderly. Snow carefully helped him to his feet. By that time, Klaus had reached the pen, too. Snow's shout had alerted him.

'I think he's hurt,' Snow said to Klaus. 'Let me see,' she said to Benjamin, trying to get a peek at his arm.

Benjamin shook her off. 'Get me away from that horse,' he said. He darted out of the pen. Moonsilver stood back, watching the scene calmly, as though he hadn't been spooked only moments before.

'Come, Princess,' Klaus said to her urgently, leading her out of the riding pen. 'Your father wouldn't want you so close to danger.'

Benjamin stalked towards the stables, ahead of his father and Snow. 'That horse is useless!' Benjamin yelled at her when he got there. 'Wherever he's from, he should go back there!'

Snow was stunned. 'It's not his fault you frightened him!'

'He's wild, Princess. And if he runs away, I won't stop him!' Benjamin continued his angry march towards the stables.

Klaus patted her on the back. 'He's just sore, little one. Sore in body and sore in pride. He doesn't mean that.'

Snow turned to the stable master, the man she trusted before anyone else — even

her father—to know what a horse was thinking, what a horse needed. 'Do you think Moonsilver is hopeless, Klaus? Do you think he can be tamed?'

Snow knew Klaus wouldn't lie to her. One of the reasons her father valued him so much as his stable master was his honesty, in addition to his skill and hard work. 'Well, Princess,' Klaus said, 'we don't know where Moonsilver came from. He has a special bond with you, which may mean he's less wild than Benjamin thinks.'

'But if he isn't wild, that would mean he belongs to someone else,' Snow said. She'd been hoping that wasn't the case.

'Horses are mighty intelligent creatures. If he belongs elsewhere, he'll be sure to let you know. But I suspect he found his way to you for a reason.'

'I hope so,' Snow said solemnly.

'Why don't you let me see to Moonsilver today,' Klaus said. Snow began to object, but Klaus continued. 'I know, I know, it's your responsibility. But I'd feel more comfortable if I took him in from the pen, considering what just happened. All right with you?'

'All right,' Snow said. She suddenly felt very tired. *Perhaps it wouldn't be such a bad thing for Moonsilver to have a little break—and for me to have one, too,* she thought.

'Thanks, Klaus,' she said. 'Will you give Moonsilver an extra apple from me? He didn't mean to hurt Benjamin.'

'Of course,' Klaus answered. 'And don't you worry. Moonsilver will be here tomorrow. I'll make sure of that myself.'

Chapter 8
A Different Way

On her way back to the castle, Snow stopped by the wishing well again. This time, she knew what she wanted to say.

'*I'm wishing,*' Snow sang. She waited for the echo.

'*I'm wishing,*' the well repeated.

'*For Benjamin to heal soon,*' she continued. The well echoed her words. '*And that he will forgive Moonsilver.*'

She paused, listening to her wish repeated. '*But most of all,*' Snow sang on.

'*Most of all.*'

'*I wish to understand Moonsilver.*'

'*I wish to understand Moonsilver.*'

The wish has to work, Snow thought. She wouldn't give up on her horse.

That night, Snow dreamed she was riding Moonsilver through open golden pastures. The pace was leisurely, with Moonsilver stopping to graze and Snow singing loud and free, her voice carried on the wind. They were a team, working together to bring home any injured animals they found. It was as if the two had been bonded for years.

When Snow awoke, the feeling in the dream stayed with her. And she saw that the key to understanding Moonsilver was something beyond training. *Love*, Snow thought. Moonsilver needed what every person and every creature in the world needed: love. And that was what she would show him.

Over breakfast, Snow's father asked her about what had happened during training the day before. His moustache twitched the way it always did when he was troubled but trying not to show it. It seemed Klaus had paid him a visit and filled him in.

'You don't need to worry, Father,' Snow

said. 'I realised something this morning.'

'Oh?' her father asked.

'Moonsilver has been nothing but gentle with me. He trusted me to find him and bring him home. Benjamin meant well, but he didn't trust Moonsilver. He didn't listen to what Moonsilver wanted.'

'How can you listen to a horse?' her father asked.

'You have to learn their language,' Snow said.

'And what language does Moonsilver speak?'

Snow White winked. 'Apples.'

Before she left the castle, Snow stopped

by the kitchens and gathered fruit in her apron.

When she reached the stables, Benjamin was pitching hay with his right hand. His left arm was in a sling. Snow stopped at the sight of him: if his arm was still injured, perhaps her wishes hadn't come true!

Benjamin saw Snow watching him and scowled. 'Don't get all worked up. Nothing's broken.' He flailed his arm around in the sling and rolled his eyes. 'My dad's making me wear this. It *barely* hurts.'

Snow grinned. That sounded like the Benjamin she knew. And that meant he must be feeling better.

Benjamin turned back to the hay and Snow grabbed another pitchfork to help. 'My dad said I should apologise to you,' he said.

'You don't need to do that,' Snow said. 'But I accept your apology.'

'I'm not apologising!' he protested. 'Your horse is out of control. That's not my fault.'

Snow laughed. 'Father is coming down to visit in a few hours. By the time he gets here, I think I'll be riding Moonsilver.' She dug her pitchfork into the hay. 'Without falling off,' she added.

'You can't,' Benjamin said. 'It's not safe.'

'Don't worry,' Snow said. 'I won't ride him if it doesn't feel safe.'

'Okay,' Benjamin said. Then he laughed,

 too. 'Moonsilver won't let you ride him, anyway. I'm not worried.'

They wheeled the wagon into the stalls and began feeding the horses in silence. After a while, Benjamin spoke again. 'I guess I am sorry, though.'

'You are?' Snow asked.

'Yeah,' Benjamin said. 'I wanted to prove that I'm ready for more than just handing out hay and mucking stalls and stuff. I thought if I could tame Moonsilver, everyone would be impressed. But I failed.'

Snow tossed her handful of hay into Doppel and Ganger's stall. 'You didn't fail! I would still trust you with any horse, including Moonsilver.' She pointed to Frost, who was hanging over her stall, watching them talk. 'Haven't you seen how much Frost adores you?'

Benjamin blushed. 'That's another thing. I guess I hoped that if I got Moonsilver up to your father's standards, maybe . . .' He drifted off without finishing his thought.

'Maybe what?' Snow asked.

'That maybe he'd let me race Frost.'

Immediately after he said it, he hung his head low, like he was ashamed.

'Why, that's a wonderful idea!' Snow said.

'You think so?' Benjamin replied, surprised.

'You have no idea how much I do *not* want to race Frost, or Moonsilver, or any horse at all! It would be so nice for my father if someone else showed interest.'

Snow clasped her hands to her chest. She had a brilliant idea. 'Benjamin, have you ever visited the wishing well?'

Benjamin snorted. 'That's just an old story,' he said. But when they were done, Snow saw him heading towards the courtyard. She smiled to herself. If he wasn't ready to tell the king or Klaus about his wish just yet, the wishing well would surely take care of his dream to race Frost.

After Benjamin was gone, Snow decided it was time to test out her new plan for Moonsilver. 'I'm glad you're still here,' she said to the horse. Moonsilver was chomping on his breakfast hay.

'Do you really want hay? Or do you want one of these?' Snow held out an apple. Moonsilver lifted his head from the hay and hung it over the stall door near Snow's hand.

'You have to let me take you out first,' she said. 'Then you can have the apple.'

Moonsilver followed Snow outside. Snow made sure to take the horse in the opposite direction from Klaus. She didn't want anyone to disturb them.

When Snow was sure they were out of view, she stopped. Moonsilver had followed her easily, without complaint. Snow held out the apple and the horse took a few gentle bites. She stroked his mane tenderly.

'I think you and I understand each other,' Snow said. 'I shouldn't have doubted that. I only wanted what was best for you, and I thought Benjamin could help.'

The horse was focused on the apple, but Snow was sure he was listening to her.

'You trusted me from the beginning, and I should have had more trust in you. Do you forgive me?'

Moonsilver took the last bite and nuzzled against her hand. Snow took this as a sign that he did, indeed, forgive her.

'There's another apple for you if you let me near your back. Okay?' Snow led the horse to some overturned crates. She stacked a couple on top of each other, making a simple stool.

Snow fetched another apple from her apron. 'I'm going to climb up next to you

now,' she said, showing him the apple. She stood on the crates and rubbed his back. Moonsilver stayed steady and calm. He didn't seem to mind her there at all.

Confident that she and Moonsilver were communicating, Snow climbed down from the crates and gave him a few bites of the apple, then led him around in a few easy circles. Again, he followed her without any trouble.

Snow grabbed a blanket and led the horse back to the crates. She began singing to him softly as she draped the blanket over his back. Snow put all her love, care and respect for Moonsilver into her voice. She hoped her methods would work better than Benjamin's.

Snow took a deep breath. 'Now, take the rest of the apple, and when you're done with it, I'm going to get on your back. Okay?'

Moonsilver continued to eat the apple, which Snow took as a yes. She stroked Moonsilver's back. And when he was finished chewing, she put the bridle she'd brought with her on him. Then she climbed up on the crates and lifted one leg up and over the blanket. Moonsilver stayed quiet. Snow let her other leg leave the crates, so she was now sitting on Moonsilver properly. Snow took the reins.

'If you want me to get down, just neigh,' Snow whispered into Moonsilver's ears. 'Otherwise, let's take a walk.'

Snow relaxed the reins. Moonsilver began to walk. Snow tried to keep her excitement under control. She didn't want to scare Moonsilver, but she was doing it! She was riding!

Moonsilver walked slowly, as if he was testing the waters himself—testing how their riding partnership would be. 'That's a good boy,' Snow cooed to the horse.

Her words seemed to give the horse confidence. He picked up the pace to a slow trot. They were getting further from the stables now. Snow was thinking she ought to try to steer Moonsilver back when she saw her father walking down from the castle. She perked up and waved to the king in the distance.

Snow changed her mind about heading back to the stables. 'Look,' she said to the horse excitedly, 'there's Father! Let's go see him.'

Moonsilver picked up his pace again, going from a trot to a canter, and then from a canter to a full gallop.

But to Snow's surprise, he galloped right past the king, towards the castle walls—towards the forest.

'Wait!' Snow cried. She looked over her shoulder. Her father was chasing them. Benjamin appeared, too, running out from the courtyard to see what was happening.

But Moonsilver was moving too quickly now. They would never catch up.

The castle wall was coming up fast. Snow closed her eyes as Moonsilver jumped.

Chapter 9
Chasing Moonsilver

Moonsilver leaped over the wall and landed gracefully on the other side. But he didn't stop running.

Snow was thankful she hadn't fallen off, but her mind was racing. Maybe Moonsilver was running back into the wilderness—and Snow had been silly enough to believe all he needed was a little love and some apples and everything would be all right.

She gripped the reins tightly. She reminded herself that she and Moonsilver were bonded—that she owed him trust, as he had trusted her. So she tried to relax her body, knowing that if she fought, she or Moonsilver—or both—could end up hurt.

'I hope you know where you're going,' she told the horse as they flew through the forest, past the spot where Snow had found him injured only two days earlier.

After several minutes of running, Snow and Moonsilver broke through a line of trees and into farmland. Snow was relieved. Farms meant people—people who were a part of her kingdom.

Moonsilver slowed down to a trot and turned sharply. He was making a beeline towards one farm in particular.

'Where are you taking us?' Snow asked. A ball of panic welled in her throat as she realised that Moonsilver must be taking her to his home. Perhaps he wasn't wild. And perhaps he didn't belong to her after all. Perhaps he never had.

Snow felt her heart quietly breaking as they got closer to the farm. She didn't want to let Moonsilver go. She'd only just found him.

At the farm's fence, Moonsilver stopped.

'Is this where I ought to say goodbye?'

Snow asked him, confused. But then she noticed two other horses approaching from within the farm. They were weak. Moonsilver  blew air through his nose in greeting and the other two horses did the same.

'Are these your friends?' Snow asked. She used the fence to climb down from Moonsilver's back into the yard. They were near a gate, and Snow let Moonsilver in. They took a walk around the grounds, searching for the farmer. The two new horses loped behind her. There was no farmer that Snow could see, but there were a few pigs, along with some cows, chickens and sheep. All the animals were terribly thin.

Suddenly, Snow realised what was going on. She stared at Moonsilver, his white crescent moon glowing in the sunlight. 'You aren't wild,' she said. 'You ran away from here . . . you ran away to get help. And you found me.'

Moonsilver snorted and nuzzled into Snow's apron. Snow retrieved an apple, but Moonsilver didn't take it. Instead, he looked at the other two horses. Snow fought back tears, understanding that Moonsilver wanted her to give the apple, his favourite treat, to his hungry friends. She dug out another apple and gave them one each.

'Princess!'

Snow turned to see Benjamin shouting for her, galloping *fast* on Frost's back towards the farm, one hand holding the reins while his other arm bounced at his side in the sling. She didn't think she'd ever seen anything move so fast, not even her father on Champion. 'I'm alright,' she called back, waving to him.

Benjamin and Frost reached the fence, and Benjamin hopped off the horse, then quickly secured her to a post. He leaped over the fence and ran to Snow. 'What happened?'

he asked, taking in the sight of Snow, the three horses and the farm.

But before Snow could answer, someone called out from the farmhouse. 'Clarence!'

'Clarence?' Benjamin and Snow repeated, confused.

An old man in tattered clothes, who seemed as thin as the animals, was slowly walking across the field. 'You found my Clarence,' the man said in a shaky voice.

Moonsilver left Snow's side, heading towards the old farmer. The man beamed at him. 'Clarence!' He patted Moonsilver's shoulder affectionately, leaning on him and catching his breath. Snow gaped at them.

But then the farmer's eyes widened. He kneeled. 'Your Majesty!'

Benjamin and Snow turned back to the fence. Snow's father was riding towards the farm, with Klaus following.

The king jumped Champion over the fence and leaped down from the horse to put a strong arm around his daughter. 'Are you alright?' he asked her.

'Yes, Father,' Snow answered. She looked at Moonsilver and the farmer. 'But I don't think everything is alright on this farm.'

Chapter 10
Handing Over the Reins

Once the king saw that Snow was safe and unthreatened by Moonsilver, he relaxed. Klaus tied Horace next to Frost and joined them.

The stable master observed the condition of the two new horses. 'These horses are underweight, Your Majesty. They need attention—soon.'

Snow's father eyed the farmer, who was

still kneeling. 'Good sir,' he said, 'please stand. Can you explain the condition of these animals?'

Snow noticed the man straighten his back slowly as though he was in pain. 'I'm ashamed to have Your Highness see this. Clarence has always been the real leader of this farm. He must have realised sooner than I did that we needed help, and ran off to find it.'

'Clarence is Moonsilver,' Snow explained to her father.

'My daughter has grown quite fond of Clarence,' the king said. 'We found him injured and hungry in the forest.' The king surveyed the rest of the farm. 'And it seems he's not the only animal in this sorry state.'

'What happened?' Snow asked. The farmer struck Snow as a gentle, caring man. *How could he have let his animals go hungry?* she wondered.

'I've grown old, Princess,' the man said. 'Running a farm alone is hard work. I had a nasty fall about a month back, and I haven't been able to get around much since. Haven't been able to take care of my chores like I used to.' The man couldn't meet their eyes. He was addressing Moonsilver instead. 'I'm very sorry,' he said. 'I'm very sorry,' he repeated, almost a whisper this time.

Snow's heart ached for the farmer. And it ached for Moonsilver and the rest of the animals there.

'What is your name, sir?' the king asked the farmer.

'Huber, Your Majesty. Paul Huber.'

The king's mouth dropped open in surprise. 'Not *the* Paul Huber? Paul Huber who used to ride Flying Fiona?'

Snow and Benjamin shared a look. *Who?* they both mouthed.

'One and the same,' Mr Huber answered sheepishly.

The king stumbled over his words. 'Why—I—I used to . . . watch you race. You

were the greatest champion the kingdom had seen until . . .'

'Until you came along,' Mr Huber finished.

'Well, yes,' the king said with a modest smile. 'I always wondered why you stopped racing.'

Mr Huber shook his head. 'My beloved Fiona couldn't race anymore. I hoped her colt would follow in her footsteps, but he hated racing. And I was already too old then, with no rider to take over for me anyhow.'

'Where's Fiona's colt now?' Snow asked.

'Well, you know him as Moonsilver,' Mr Huber answered.

Snow was in awe. A racehorse's offspring with no interest in racing. She and Moonsilver had even more in common than she'd realised!

'So let's see here,' Klaus chimed in. 'We have a racehorse who doesn't want to race, a racehorse who was born to race'—he pointed at Frost—'a master rider with no-one to train, and a farm full of animals who need care.' Klaus raised his eyebrows at the king. The king nodded as though he knew what Klaus was thinking.

'Mr Huber,' the king said, 'what would you say to moving into the castle and training the next champion racer?'

Snow's heart sank. *Oh, no*, she thought. She had to speak up before it was too late.

But to her surprise, the king put his arm around Benjamin. 'I think this boy is going to be faster than you or I could have ever dreamed of being.'

Benjamin's face lit up in surprise. 'Me?' he asked.

'I've seen the way you are with Frost,' the king said. 'And the fact that you beat me here— one-handed, no less—was very impressive!'

'I'm honoured, Your Majesty.' Benjamin bowed his head.

'As am I,' Mr Huber said. 'But what will become of my animals?'

The king hesitated.

'Leave them to me,' Snow White piped up. 'We can bring them to the castle, can't we, Father? I know just what they need.'

'And what's that?' the king asked.

Snow smiled up at him. 'Good food, a clean, warm place to sleep and love, of course.'

Her father laughed. 'Of course,' he repeated. 'It sounds like you do know just what they need!' He turned to Mr Huber. 'We have plenty of room at the castle. They'll be in excellent hands.'

Snow threw her arms around her father's waist. 'Thank you, Father,' she breathed into his robes. 'Thank you.'

It took several trips and the use of a few royal wagons to transport all the animals and Mr Huber's possessions to the castle. Moonsilver trotted along with a new bounce in his step. He hopped around playfully as his fellow farm animals entered the royal stables. Mr Huber had agreed without question that not only should Snow be the one to care for his animals, but Moonsilver should remain her horse—and keep his new name.

Klaus and the king led Mr Huber up to the castle to introduce him to the rest of the staff while Snow and Benjamin worked together to get all the animals settled into their new homes.

'I guess your wishing well worked,' Benjamin said as they put out some food for the very grateful pigs.

'I told you,' Snow said. 'The well is magic.'

'So is the way you got that horse to listen to you,' Benjamin said. 'I couldn't do that.'

Snow shrugged. 'And I couldn't get Frost to listen to me. So we'll both just stick to what we know for a while. Deal?'

Benjamin grinned. 'It's a deal, Princess.'

'Oh, and one more thing . . .' Snow added.

'What's that?' Benjamin asked.

'Call me Snow.'

'You got it . . . Snow.'

They finished up with the pigs before moving on to the sheep. Moonsilver and Frost whinnied from their stalls as Benjamin and Snow passed.

The two friends stopped to give each horse an apple and a loving pat on the nose. As Snow stroked Moonsilver's crescent marking, she thought about the wonderful days ahead that would be spent caring for these animals while Benjamin was training to race, guided by her father and Mr Huber.

It seemed everyone had gotten what they wished for—animals and humans alike.